I0830772

SWAGGER WARS II ™

Her Turn ™

Not Bossy. Just Bold. ™

Author - Joyce Lee

ISBN Hardback: 979-8-9930206-8-6

Library of Congress Control Number: 2025922048

Text copyright 2025 by Joyce Lee

Illustration copyright 2025 by Umair Ali

Swagger Wars II™ Her Turn™ and the tagline *Not Bossy. Just Bold*™ are trademarks of **Spirit, Inc.**, a 501(c)(3) nonprofit organization based in Texas.

Published by **Spirit, Inc.**

Houston, Texas | www.spirit-np.info

Cover Design by Umair Ali

Interior Design by Umair Ali

First Edition – 2025

Printed in the United States of America

10 9 8 7 6 5 4 3 2 1

Dedicated to:

For every young female finding her strength,

her confidence,

and her place in the world.

For those who lead with heart,

rise after the fall,

and never stop showing up for themselves.

May you always remember—

you are enough,

you are capable,

and it's finally **Her Turn.**

— **Joyce Lee**

"Owning the Court"

The court was never built for me,
they said it was his space, his noise, his name.
But sneakers don't care who laces them first,
and hardwood remembers every flame.

Swagger isn't loud; it's steady,
a heartbeat that refuses to fade.
It's showing up when the room forgets you,
and leaving proof you played.

They can guard the rim, block the lane,
call me too much, too proud, too strong—
but every young female who's ever been benched knows:
this game has always been ours all along.

\-   **Joyce Lee**

CONTENTS

Part I: Breaking the Mold 9

    Chapter One: The Court Is His, Not Hers 11

    Chapter 2: Benched Swagger .17

    Chapter 3: Locker Room Whispers 23

    Chapter 4: Coach's Rules, Maya's Fire 29

Part II: The Pressure Zone 35

    Chapter 5: Invisible or Too Much 37

    Chapter 6: Playing Through Pain 43

    Chapter 7: Sisterhood on the Line. 49

    Chapter 8: Swagger Costs 55

    Chapter 9: The Underdog Game 63

    Chapter 10: Her Turn to Lead. 69

    Chapter 11: Respect, Not Permission 75

    Chapter 12: Swagger Redefined. 83

    Author's Note. 91

    About the Author. 93

PART I:

BREAKING THE MOLD

CHAPTER ONE

THE COURT IS HIS, NOT HERS

The squeak of sneakers split the air like static. The gym's fluorescent lights buzzed overhead, washing the court in that familiar yellow haze that made every scuff mark shine. Boys darted back and forth beneath the glow, shouting, laughing, and calling plays that echoed through the rafters. Their voices rolled across the empty bleachers, filling every inch of the place that Maya once thought belonged to her.

She leaned against the cool brick wall, hoodie pulled low over her ponytail, basketball wedged tight against her side. The air smelled of rubber, polish, and sweat — her favorite combination — but tonight it felt different. The gym used to feel like home. Now it felt like enemy territory.

One of the boys, a tall guard with a loose grin, glanced her way. "Hey, Maya, you lost? Girls' team practices down the hall."

The others snickered. Not cruelly — just casually, the kind of laughter that came easy to people who never had to question if they belonged.

Maya smirked, even though something in her chest tightened. "Funny," she said, pushing off the wall. "I came to show you how it's done."

That got a few louder laughs. Another boy spun the ball on his finger like he was on TV. "Nah, this is real ball. Not JV warm-ups."

She gripped her own ball tighter. No matter how many hours she practiced, no matter how crisp her jumper or tight her crossover, she always had to prove it twice. Boys could swagger onto the court and be called confident. When she did it, they called it attitude.

Coach Ramirez's words from last week echoed in her head: *Watch your tone, Maya. No one likes a girl who acts like she's in charge.*

She'd nodded at the time, but the words had burned since. Why was it swagger when Darius yelled at a ref, but a "bad attitude" when she spoke up? Why was Malik's fire "leadership," but hers "drama"?

Maya tugged off her hoodie, letting her ponytail fall against her neck. The air cooled her arms, and the sound of bouncing balls buzzed in her ears like a dare. She bounced her own ball once, twice. *Thud, thud.* The sound echoed sharp across the gym.

"Check ball," she said flatly, stepping onto the hardwood.

The laughter paused. A few boys exchanged looks; one raised an eyebrow. "You sure you want to run with us?"

"Unless you're scared."

That did it. The teasing turned to murmurs of challenge. A game started forming before anyone even agreed to it — because swagger, real swagger, was contagious.

They gave her the ball first, maybe as a joke. One pass. One dribble. A quick crossover. She sliced between two defenders before they even blinked and kissed the ball gently off the glass. *Swish.*

The laughter stopped.

Next possession, she read their eyes, cut a passing lane, and snatched the ball clean. Her shoes burned against the floor as she sprinted down-court. Two steps, pull-up jumper, perfect arc. Nothing but net.

Someone muttered, "She just got lucky."

Maya didn't answer. She jogged back on defense, ponytail swinging like a flag. Her game spoke louder than anything she could say.

She knew what would come — the excuses, the whispers. They'd call it flukes or say she got "hot." No matter how many shots she made, they'd find a reason it didn't count.

Not yet, anyway.

She dribbled slow and steady, heartbeat syncing to the rhythm. Swagger wasn't jewelry or talk. Swagger was this: skill, confidence, and consistency when no one believed you could keep it up.

Darius, the tallest boy on the court, grinned as he wiped sweat from his forehead. "Alright, Maya. You got moves. But you can't hang for a whole game."

Maya raised her chin. "We'll see."

The ball snapped back into play. The boys doubled her immediately — hands swiping, shoulders pressing in. She pivoted, spun out of their trap, and fired a no-look pass that sliced between defenders. Her teammate missed the layup, but Maya smiled. That wasn't the point. The point was *control.*

Now they looked at her differently. Not all of them, but enough. She could feel it — that crack in the wall. Respect trying to seep through.

Minutes turned into sweat and breath. Her lungs burned, her arms ached, but she didn't slow down. Every bucket, every steal, chipped away at the doubt around her.

The scoreboard didn't matter. The empty bleachers didn't matter. What mattered was that, for once, the boys had to *look at her* — really look. Not as a girl invading their court, but as a baller.

The ball hit the floor again, steady as a heartbeat. Her body moved on instinct — cross, pivot, pull-up, release. The sound of the net was the only applause she needed.

The game grew quieter. No more jokes. No more smirks. Just sneakers and breath and the sound of effort.

That silence? That was respect.

But Maya knew it wouldn't last outside this gym. Tomorrow, someone would say she got lucky. Coaches would still tell her to "tone it down." Someone would remind her that swagger looked better on boys.

She inhaled deep, tasting the salt in the air. Let them talk. Let them doubt.

After the game, she sat alone on the bleachers, towel draped around her shoulders. The gym lights flickered overhead, humming low. Darius passed by, dribbling lazily, and nodded. "You can play, Harper. For real."

Maya almost smiled. "Told you."

He grinned, half-impressed, half-unwilling to admit it. "Guess we'll see next time."

She watched him go, the echo of his sneakers fading down the hall. For the first time that night, the gym was quiet. The kind of quiet that felt earned.

Her palms still tingled from gripping the ball. Her knees ached. She didn't care. Every bruise tonight meant something. Every drop of sweat rewrote a rule that said she didn't belong.

Maya stood, walking back to center court. She bounced the ball once. The sound filled the empty space like a promise.

This was her reminder: the game would never hand her anything. Not respect, not recognition, not room. She'd have to take it — shot by shot, breath by breath.

She looked up at the scoreboard one last time. It wasn't even turned on. No points, no clock, no proof that tonight had happened.

But Maya knew better.

She'd earned something more than numbers.

She'd made the court remember her.

That night, lying in bed, the rhythm of the game replayed in her head — the bounce, the breath, the silence after each swish. Somewhere between exhaustion and satisfaction, she smiled.

Swagger, she realized, wasn't loud. It wasn't about showing off or shutting people up. It was the quiet confidence to step onto a court where no one thinks you belong and make them see you anyway.

Tomorrow she'd lace up again. Same court. Same whispers. Same double standards.

But this time, she'd bring more than a basketball.

She'd bring proof.

And that, Maya decided, was her kind of swagger.

CHAPTER 2

BENCHED SWAGGER

By the next afternoon, the gym smelled like polish and sweat, but the energy felt heavy. The boys were gone now. It was the girls' turn — maroon jerseys lined up, ponytails swinging, sneakers squeaking in neat rows.

Coach Ramirez paced the sideline with her whistle spinning on its cord. Every few steps, she stopped, crossed her arms, and scanned the court like she was searching for something none of them had yet found.

Maya bounced her ball between her knees, the rhythm steady and sharp. She still felt the high from last night's game — the adrenaline, the silence after her last shot, the way Darius had said, *You can play, Harper.* But she knew it wouldn't matter here. Not with Coach Ramirez. Not with the team that didn't see what she was fighting against.

"Alright, ladies, bring it in!" Coach barked.

The circle tightened. Sneakers squeaked, balls thudded once before falling still.

"We've got Northside this weekend," Coach said, pacing in front of them. "They're fast, they're aggressive, and they play clean. I want discipline. I want composure. Swagger's fine for them—" she jerked her thumb toward the boys' locker room "—but for us? We need control. We don't need attitude making us look sloppy."

The words hit Maya like static through her chest. Swagger's fine for them. Not for us.

Coach's gaze flicked her way. "Maya, you listening?"

"Yes, Coach," she said, voice even.

Coach narrowed her eyes, like she could hear the fire behind the calm. "Good. You've got talent, no doubt. But sometimes you're… too much. This team doesn't need show-boats. It needs chemistry."

The circle shifted — sneakers scraping the floor, glances traded. Some teammates stared at the ground. Others peeked sideways at Maya, curious to see if she'd explode.

Too much. There it was again. The label she couldn't shake.

Maya bit the inside of her cheek, jaw tight. "Yes, Coach."

Coach nodded. "Good. Let's run drills."

The whistle cut the air, sharp as a blade.

They broke into pairs for passing drills. Maya ended up with Janelle, a quiet sopho-more with quick feet and soft eyes that avoided confrontation.

"Don't take it personal," Janelle whispered as they chest-passed. "Coach just wants everyone calm."

Maya caught the ball and fired it back a little harder than she meant to. "I *was* calm," she said. "Why's playing hard always a problem?"

Janelle shrugged. "Because it's you. You stand out."

Maya didn't answer. She just dribbled harder. Stand out. People said it like a compli-ment, but it never meant one. It meant *too loud, too confident, too visible.*

When scrimmage time came, Maya flipped a switch. Her body moved before her thoughts caught up — muscle memory from hours in empty gyms. She stole passes, cut through defenders, and barked out rotations. Her game had rhythm, bite, control.

But every time she shouted a direction or clapped her hands to reset the play, Coach's whistle screamed.

"Tone it down, Maya!"

"Quit barking orders!"

"Let someone else lead!"

By the third interruption, the burn in Maya's throat wasn't from yelling — it was from swallowing the words she wanted to throw back.

Finally, after she intercepted a sloppy pass and took it coast to coast for a clean layup, the whistle blasted again.

"Bench, Maya. Now."

The gym froze.

"What? Coach, I—"

"Bench!"

Maya's face flushed. She stormed toward the sideline, towel clenched tight in her hands. The bench felt colder than usual, its wood pressing against her legs like punishment. She stared at the court as her teammates stumbled through possessions without her — missed layups, bad passes, empty energy.

Coach didn't call her back in. Not once.

When practice finally ended, the team collapsed around center court, panting. Sweat darkened their jerseys, and the sound of heavy breathing filled the space.

"Good work," Coach said, pacing again. "Except for the attitudes. This isn't about stars; it's about a team."

Her eyes flicked to Maya like a period at the end of a sentence.

Nobody said anything. The only sound was sneakers scuffing as players drifted toward the locker room.

Janelle gave Maya a quick, apologetic glance before looking away.

Maya stayed seated after everyone left, gripping her basketball so tightly it squeaked. The sound echoed through the empty gym.

She'd been taught to work twice as hard to earn half the respect. She could handle that. But being told to shrink — that cut deeper than any loss.

The doors creaked, and Coach Ramirez reappeared, clipboard tucked under her arm. She stopped a few feet away, crossing her arms.

"You've got talent," she said quietly. "But talent without control? It burns out fast."

Maya didn't look up. "Why is it swagger when the boys yell, but attitude when I do? Why do they get to lead, but I get told to sit down?"

Coach sighed, leaning on the bleachers. "Life's not fair, Maya. You play too loud, people notice. You play too quiet, they forget you. You've got to learn to walk that line if you want to last."

Maya looked up, meeting her eyes. "Maybe I don't want to walk that line. Maybe I want to draw a new one."

Coach studied her for a moment, then nodded once — not agreement, but acknowledgment — and left.

The locker room steamed from the showers when Maya walked in. The air was thick with chatter and whispers that cut off the second she entered. She could feel eyes on her, could hear the quiet laughter in corners.

She sat on the bench in front of her locker, towel draped around her neck, staring at the scuffed floor. Her reflection glimmered faintly in the metal door — tired eyes, strong shoulders, and something in her posture that looked like defiance.

Maybe Coach was right. Maybe she was too much. Too vocal. Too fiery. Too visible.

But then she remembered last night — the hush when her jumper hit net, the disbelief in their eyes, the quiet nod of respect from Darius.

That wasn't too much. That was the game done right.

She grabbed her ball and stood. The chatter around her dimmed again. For a moment, she thought about saying something — explaining herself, apologizing, anything to make the silence less heavy. But she didn't owe them comfort.

She owed herself confidence.

As she walked out of the locker room, the ball bounced once against the tile. *Thud.* The sound echoed down the empty hallway like a heartbeat.

Outside, the late sun poured through the gym doors, painting the floor gold. Maya stopped in the doorway, breathing in the warm air. Her reflection shimmered faintly in the glass — a girl with tired eyes and unshaken resolve.

Swagger wasn't about how loud you talked. It was about how long you kept standing after they told you to sit.

She balanced the ball on her fingertips and whispered to herself, "They can bench me today. But they won't silence me tomorrow."

Then she stepped out into the light, the gym door closing behind her with a soft, defiant click.

CHAPTER 3

LOCKER ROOM WHISPERS

The sound of running water filled the locker room, mixing with the faint thump of music from someone's phone speaker. Steam curled through the air, carrying the scent of soap, sweat, and exhaustion. Practice was over, but the tension still hung thick, like humidity that refused to lift.

Maya sat on the wooden bench in front of her locker, towel draped across her shoulders. Her jersey clung to her back, damp from drills that had felt more like punishment than training. She'd barely spoken since Coach benched her. The silence had become its own kind of protest.

Around her, voices rose and fell in low tones—small pockets of conversation that stopped and shifted whenever she glanced up.

"Coach was tight today," one girl said.

"Yeah, well, she had to be. Some people don't know when to chill," another answered, her voice pointed, careful but sharp.

Maya's jaw tightened. *Some people.* She didn't have to ask who they meant.

A few lockers down, Janelle fiddled with her hair tie, eyes flicking between Maya and the others. She looked caught between loyalty and fear, the kind of silence that said too much.

Maya took a deep breath and tried to focus on the rhythm of the dripping faucet instead of the words being whispered. But the whispers had a way of finding her anyway.

"She acts like she's the captain or something."

"She's always talking like we can't run plays without her."

"Coach just doesn't want her messing up the team vibe."

The words slipped through the steam, small but poisonous. Each one landed like a pebble in Maya's stomach, tiny ripples of heat spreading through her chest.

She slammed her locker shut. The sound cracked through the chatter, snapping a few heads her way. "If you've got something to say," she said, voice even, "say it."

Silence.

Then a shrug from Keira, one of the starting forwards. "Nobody said your name."

"Didn't have to."

Keira crossed her arms. "You think Coach benched you for no reason? You've been doing the most since tryouts. Maybe chill a little."

Maya met her eyes. "So playing hard is doing the most?"

Keira smirked. "Playing hard is fine. Acting like the court revolves around you? That's different."

Janelle opened her mouth like she wanted to step in but didn't. The rest of the team watched, waiting to see if a storm was coming.

Maya grabbed her duffel bag and stood. "You know what's funny? None of you cared when Darius did the same thing last year. Y'all cheered him on. But I raise my voice, and suddenly it's an ego problem."

Keira rolled her eyes. "You always bringing up the boys. This is *our* team."

"Then start acting like it," Maya shot back. "Because right now, y'all sound like them."

The silence that followed wasn't victory—it was isolation. Maya felt it immediately. As she walked out, whispers began again, quiet but sharp. She didn't turn back. She didn't want to see who was smiling behind her back and who was just too afraid to look up.

Out in the hallway, the gym echoed with distant bounce drills from the JV team. The sound used to comfort her. Tonight it just felt hollow.

She found an empty row of bleachers and sat down, the cool metal biting against her skin. The gym lights had dimmed, leaving long shadows across the court. She imagined all the games that had played out here—boys yelling, coaches shouting, fans cheering. The noise had always been louder than her voice. But lately, that silence that followed her everywhere was louder still.

Her phone buzzed beside her. A text from Janelle.

Janelle: don't trip. they just jealous.

Janelle: coach will come around.

Maya stared at the screen, thumbs hovering. She wanted to believe that, but she knew better. Coach wouldn't come around. Not until Maya changed—toned it down, softened her edges. And she couldn't do that without losing the part of her that made her who she was.

She typed back:

Maya: I'm good. just tired.

Then she slipped the phone into her bag and leaned forward, elbows on knees. The echo of her heartbeat filled her ears.

The next morning, the whispers followed her into the hallways at school. Not loud, not obvious—just small enough to sting. She caught her name between giggles, between lockers slamming and shoes squeaking against tile.

"Girl thinks she's some kind of hero."

"She got benched, didn't she?"

"I heard Coach might pull her from starting."

By lunch, Maya was exhausted from pretending not to hear. She ate alone at the far end of the cafeteria, earbuds in but no music playing, just static. Janelle slid into the seat across from her with a tray and a nervous smile.

"You okay?" she asked.

Maya shrugged. "I'm used to it."

"You shouldn't have to be."

Janelle pushed a grape around her tray with a fork. "Coach is old school. She thinks being calm makes us look professional. She just doesn't want people to call us emotional."

Maya looked up. "You mean *girls*. She doesn't want people to call girls emotional."

Janelle didn't argue. She didn't have to.

For a long moment, they just sat there. The hum of cafeteria noise filled the space between them—trays clattering, voices rising and falling, the buzz of too many people talking about everything except what mattered.

Then Maya spoke quietly. "You ever feel like no matter what you do, it's wrong?"

Janelle nodded slowly. "Yeah. Especially when you're good."

Maya gave a small laugh, not bitter but tired. "Guess that makes us dangerous, huh?"

Janelle smiled. "Maybe. Or maybe it makes us leaders."

The word hung there. *Leaders.* It felt both heavy and right.

After school, Maya went back to the gym. It was empty again, the way she liked it. Late sunlight poured through the high windows, turning the court golden. Dust floated like tiny sparks in the beams of light.

She dropped her bag, picked up a ball, and started dribbling. Slow. Then faster. Crossovers, behind-the-back, spin moves. The rhythm settled her heartbeat. The sound of each bounce replaced the noise from the locker room, the cafeteria, her own head.

Thud.

Thud-thud.

Thud.

She shot. The ball hit the rim, circled, and dropped in. She caught it on the rebound and started again.

Minutes passed—maybe hours. She lost track. The game was the only place she still felt whole.

When she finally stopped, she sat cross-legged at center court, breathing hard. The silence was warm, almost forgiving. She looked around at the empty gym and whispered, "If they won't listen, I'll show them."

Her voice echoed faintly, but the sound didn't fade. It lingered, like a promise.

That night, she opened her notebook and began jotting plays. Not just the ones Coach ran, but new ones—angles that made sense, movements that fit her team's rhythm better than the stiff drills they were running. She wrote until her hand cramped, sketching out arrows and notes in the margins.

She wasn't trying to prove herself anymore. She was planning something bigger. A new way to lead.

Before she closed the notebook, she wrote one last line across the bottom of the page:

Swagger isn't noise. It's proof.

The next morning, she walked into practice with that same notebook tucked under her arm. The whispers hadn't gone anywhere, but they didn't sting this time. Let them talk.

Maya wasn't chasing approval anymore. She was building something they couldn't ignore.

CHAPTER 4

COACH'S RULES, MAYA'S FIRE

The sound of sneakers squeaking before sunrise was almost sacred. The gym lights flickered awake one by one, humming against the dawn silence. Maya stood alone at the free-throw line, sweat already gathering along her temple. She'd been there since six, chasing the rhythm that made everything else fade.

Dribble, breathe, shoot. Swish.

Dribble, breathe, shoot. Rim. Rebound.

Each repetition was both punishment and peace.

She was halfway through her third round when the door creaked open. Coach Ramirez stepped inside, clipboard in hand, coffee steaming. Her sneakers echoed softly as she crossed the court.

"You're early," Coach said.

Maya caught her breath. "Always am."

Coach stopped near the sideline, watching. "You don't waste time, I'll give you that."

"I don't have time to waste."

The words came out sharper than she meant. Coach's eyebrow lifted. "You talking to me or to yourself?"

Maya bounced the ball once, twice, keeping her eyes on the rim. "Both."

Coach exhaled through her nose, setting the clipboard on the scorer's table. "You've got drive, Harper. No one can say you don't. But drive without direction? That's how players burn out."

Maya shot again. The ball swished clean through. "Or maybe it's how players get noticed."

Coach folded her arms. "You still thinking about that benching?"

"I'm thinking about everything that led up to it."

The gym fell silent except for the buzz of the lights. Maya could feel Coach's eyes on her — steady, evaluating.

Coach finally spoke. "You think I benched you because I don't like confidence?"

Maya turned. "Didn't you?"

"I benched you," Coach said evenly, "because leadership isn't about how loud you are. It's about how long people will follow when you stop talking."

Maya frowned. "They won't follow if I stay quiet, either."

"Then you have to learn the difference between leading and performing."

That word hit like a foul. *Performing.*

"I'm not performing," Maya said. "I'm playing."

"Playing for who?"

Maya hesitated. "The team."

Coach stepped closer, lowering her voice. "Are you sure? Because sometimes, it looks like you're playing to prove a point."

Maya's hands tightened on the ball. "Maybe proving a point is the only way people notice what I can do."

"People already notice. That's the problem."

Maya's jaw clenched. "So I should make myself smaller?"

Coach sighed. "I'm saying pick your battles."

The words scraped against everything Maya believed. She'd spent years picking battles — every game, every classroom, every comment that told her to calm down. She'd been polite, patient, quiet. It hadn't gotten her anywhere.

Maya stepped closer. "You ever been told you were too much, Coach?"

Coach looked at her for a long moment. "Every day I've been in this job."

That stopped Maya.

Ramirez leaned on the wall, eyes softening. "When I started, they said a woman couldn't handle coaching varsity. Said players wouldn't respect me. So I kept my voice steady. I built credibility before I raised my volume. You can't fight every fight at once, Harper. You pick one, win it, then move to the next."

Maya studied her. The lines around Coach's eyes looked different now — not just stern but tired, the kind of tired that came from years of being the only one in the room who had to prove she belonged.

Still, Maya shook her head. "If I wait my turn, it'll never come."

Coach smiled faintly. "That's your fire talking."

"Maybe that's what we need," Maya said. "Fire. Not quiet."

Coach pushed away from the wall. "Maybe. But if you burn everything around you, what's left to lead?"

The question lingered between them. Maya didn't have an answer.

When practice started an hour later, the gym buzzed with new energy. The girls filed in, groggy and yawning, some still chewing breakfast bars. Maya was already mid-drill.

Coach clapped. "Alright, ladies, let's get to work."

They ran through passing sets, then scrimmages. Maya kept her tone even, her gestures sharp but measured. She called plays, but softer this time, almost testing the air.

Still, whispers floated behind her. "Watch her. She's trying again." "Coach better not start."

Maya ignored them. She focused on movement — the clean cut, the pivot, the timing. She didn't need to prove attitude; she needed to prove balance.

Halfway through, Janelle fumbled a pass. The ball skidded toward the sideline. Maya dove, saving it inches before it rolled out, then bounced to her knees and fired it back into play.

The whistle blew.

Coach looked at her. "Harper!"

Maya froze. "Yes, Coach?"

"Nice hustle."

The words startled her. For the first time in weeks, they weren't correction — they were praise.

The court went quiet. The other players exchanged looks. Coach didn't seem to notice; she just motioned for the game to continue.

Something in Maya's chest loosened.

She wasn't trying to be the loudest anymore. She was just playing — with control, with purpose, with quiet authority.

After practice, most of the team filed out laughing, talking about weekend plans. Maya lingered, collecting stray balls. Janelle walked over, grinning.

"Did you hear that?" she said. "Coach said nice hustle."

Maya smirked. "Yeah, I'm framing that in my locker."

"You earned it," Janelle said. Then her tone softened. "You're getting better at… you know, letting people see the leader part without the fire burning everything down."

Maya raised an eyebrow. "Fire's who I am."

"Yeah, but now it's pointed in the right direction."

Maya chuckled. "You sound like Coach."

"She's rubbing off on me. Or maybe you are."

They both laughed, and for once, the sound didn't feel like tension breaking. It felt like relief.

That evening, Maya stayed behind again. The gym lights flickered as the janitor passed by, humming. She stood at center court, holding the ball loosely in both hands.

Earlier that morning, Coach's words had sounded like limits. Now they felt like lessons — not about shrinking, but about *strategizing*.

Maybe leadership wasn't about proving herself every second. Maybe it was about knowing when to speak and when to let the game speak for her.

She looked up at the scoreboard — dark and empty — and imagined it lit with her name again. But this time, not because she fought to be noticed. Because she earned it, and others followed because they believed.

She bounced the ball once. The sound echoed through the empty space, steady and sure.

That was her rhythm. Her fire, under control but never gone.

The next day, during drills, Coach called the team into a circle.

"Northside game tomorrow," she said. "We've been sloppy on defense, and we need someone to call rotations clearly."

She paused, scanning faces. Then: "Maya, you've got the floor."

Maya blinked. "Me?"

Coach nodded. "You see the court better than most. Run it."

The circle shifted in surprise. Keira's eyebrows shot up. Janelle's face broke into a grin.

Maya took a step forward, heartbeat thundering. "Alright," she said, voice steady. "Let's set up a 2-3 zone and watch the corner gaps. No freelancing."

The girls moved instantly, their sneakers squeaking in rhythm. For the first time, they followed without side comments or smirks.

Coach watched from the sideline, arms crossed, a faint smile ghosting across her face.

When the whistle blew at the end, she said quietly, "That's leadership, Harper. Keep it."

Maya nodded, chest rising with something between relief and pride. She knew she hadn't changed overnight — she'd just learned to channel it.

Her fire wasn't gone. It was focused.

And tomorrow, when the lights came up and the stands filled, she'd be ready to show everyone what *controlled swagger* looked like.

THE PRESSURE ZONE

CHAPTER 5

INVISIBLE OR TOO MUCH

Game day always smelled like rubber soles and nerves. The bleachers were starting to fill, voices echoing high into the rafters. Bright lights cut across the polished floor like a stage.

Maya laced up her shoes slowly, the sounds of sneakers, chatter, and bouncing balls swirling around her. For once, she was starting—not just as a player, but as *floor captain*. Coach Ramirez's voice still echoed in her head from that morning's huddle:

"Lead the floor, Harper. Don't just play—guide."

She'd nodded, her heart thudding with a mix of pride and pressure.

Now, sitting at the edge of the bench with the team huddled up, that pressure felt heavier than her jersey.

Janelle leaned over, whispering, "You good?"

Maya managed a smile. "Ask me after tip-off."

"Okay, Captain," Janelle teased, bumping her shoulder.

Maya smirked, but her stomach twisted. That word—Captain—still felt borrowed, like it might be taken back at any moment.

The whistle blew.

From the first possession, Northside came fast. Their guards were smaller but quick, darting through screens like lightning. Maya called out switches, waving her teammates into place.

"Stay low, Janelle! Watch your left—cut it!"

Her voice rose above the noise, strong and sure. The rhythm of the game carried her; her fire pulsed steady beneath the surface.

By halftime, they were tied. The team huddled up, panting. Coach's clipboard rattled with quick diagrams.

"Maya, what's your read?" Coach asked.

The question caught her off guard. Coach was looking straight at her. The girls were waiting.

Maya swallowed. "They're overloading the right side. If we swing faster and cut baseline, we can pull them off balance."

Coach nodded. "You heard her. Run it."

The team nodded too—no eye rolls, no whispers. Just focus.

For a few minutes, Maya felt it—the thing she'd been chasing since the first day she stepped on this court. Leadership that wasn't forced, wasn't questioned, just *respected.*

But the second half told a different story.

The crowd got louder. Northside tightened up their defense, and the game turned into chaos. Passes went wild, tempers flared, and fatigue crept in.

Maya barked orders, trying to keep the team together. "Talk! Talk on defense! Rotate!"

Then Keira snapped. "Stop yelling, Maya! We can hear you!"

Maya froze mid-play. The ball flew past her, and Northside scored.

The whistle shrieked. Coach called timeout.

As the team huddled, the air felt tight with frustration. Keira crossed her arms, breathing hard. "She's not the only one out here, Coach."

Maya stared at her. "I'm calling plays. That's my job."

"Your job ain't to act like a coach!" Keira snapped.

Coach held up a hand. "Enough." She looked at both of them. "Keira, control your temper. Maya, bring your volume down. Lead with composure, not commands."

The timeout buzzer sounded before either of them could respond. The team scattered back to the court, and Maya's chest burned.

Composure, not commands.

But what good was composure if no one listened unless she yelled?

When the game ended, they'd lost by four. The scoreboard glared like a wound.

The team filed into the locker room, sweaty and silent. Coach followed last, clipboard under her arm. She spoke without turning.

"We'll talk Monday."

Then she left.

As soon as the door shut, the murmurs started.

"Coach only blamed her because she's the loudest."

"She's got that main character energy."

"She's just mad we lost."

Maya sat on the bench, staring at the floor. The sound of zippers, Velcro, and running water filled the space. Each comment sank deeper.

She'd done what Coach asked—led, called plays, organized—but somehow it still wasn't right. Too quiet, and no one followed. Too loud, and she was bossy. She was either invisible or too much.

Janelle sat down next to her, silent at first. Then, softly, "You didn't do anything wrong."

"Didn't do anything right either," Maya muttered.

"You can't win with people who've already decided what you're supposed to be."

Maya sighed. "Feels like that's everybody."

Janelle's voice was low but certain. "Then stop trying to fit it. Be whatever makes you win."

That night, Maya couldn't sleep. She lay in bed staring at the ceiling, the scoreboard burned into her mind. She kept hearing the whispers, the criticism, the moments where she almost had the team and then lost them again.

Her notebook sat open on her desk, the same one she'd been sketching plays in. She picked it up and flipped to a blank page.

At the top, she wrote in block letters:

What does leadership really look like?

She stared at it for a long time. Then she started writing:

It's not yelling.

It's not silence.

It's knowing when your team needs one or the other.

It's being seen for the right reasons, not just heard.

It's showing up when they expect you to fall back.

Her handwriting was messy, rushed, but it felt right. She paused, the pen hovering over the page, then added one more line:

It's not about proving I belong. It's about *playing like I already do.*

On Monday, practice felt different. The gym lights buzzed overhead, but the tension from Friday still hung in the air.

Coach gathered them at center court. "We should've won that game," she said. "But we didn't because we lost focus. We don't play as individuals. We play as a team."

Her gaze met Maya's. For a heartbeat, Maya expected another lecture. But Coach surprised her.

"Harper," she said, "you've got instincts I trust. Use them—but know when to let others lead too."

Maya nodded, the words settling differently this time.

"Yes, Coach."

During drills, Maya kept her energy calm but steady. She didn't yell; she communicated. When Keira hit a jumper, Maya clapped and called, "Nice shot." When Janelle missed a rotation, Maya corrected her without attitude.

The shift was small, but the team felt it. The air started to loosen.

Midway through practice, Coach called out, "Run the Northside break! Maya, lead it!"

Maya took the ball, eyes scanning the floor. The girls fell into rhythm—clean passes, quick cuts, voices overlapping in sync. The play clicked perfectly, ending with Janelle sinking a layup.

The whistle blew.

Coach smiled faintly. "That's the balance. Remember that."

After practice, as everyone filed out, Maya lingered again, wiping her face with a towel. The gym was empty except for the echo of bouncing balls from the JV court down the hall.

She thought about all the things she'd been called: loud, bossy, dramatic. And all the things she hadn't: leader, mentor, captain.

Maybe the difference wasn't in the words themselves—it was in who said them and how she carried them.

If they were going to label her anyway, she might as well define what the label meant.

She looked up at the empty bleachers, imagining them full, imagining the noise, the energy, the weight.

Then she whispered under her breath, "I'm not too much. I'm just enough for what's coming."

Her voice carried across the court, soft but certain.

And for the first time in a long time, it didn't echo back.

It stayed.

CHAPTER 6

PLAYING THROUGH PAIN

The gym lights seemed harsher that morning. Each bounce of the basketball hit the floor like a heartbeat, echoing through Maya's head. The Northside loss still sat heavy in her stomach, and she was determined to shake it off.

She arrived early, as usual, before the rest of the team. The air still smelled of wax and polish. She took her spot at the top of the key and began her routine—one dribble, cross, step-back jumper.

Swish.

Again.

Swish.

The sound calmed her. It was proof that she still had control of something, even if everything else felt shaky.

She went for another drive, pushing harder this time, and when her right foot landed, her ankle rolled.

The pain was instant—a hot sting that shot through her leg. She stumbled, caught herself on the baseline, and froze.

For a moment, she couldn't breathe. Then she hissed through her teeth, gripping the wall.

"Not now," she whispered.

By the time the team filed in, Maya was sitting on the bench, laces loosened, ankle swelling beneath her sock.

Coach Ramirez spotted her immediately. "What happened?"

"Just tweaked it," Maya said quickly. "I'm fine."

Coach crouched down, frowning. "You don't look fine. You need to ice that."

"I can still go."

"Maya." The tone in Coach's voice wasn't up for debate.

Maya clenched her jaw, but nodded. She pulled the ice pack from the med kit and pressed it to her ankle, pretending it didn't sting like fire.

The rest of the team began warm-ups. Sneakers squeaked, laughter echoed. Maya sat still, every muscle in her body begging to move.

She hated this feeling—watching.

Janelle jogged by and whispered, "You'll be back in no time."

Maya smiled, but it felt tight. "Yeah."

By mid-practice, she'd learned that sitting still hurt worse than running. Every play, every cut, every pass—her mind followed them like she was still out there. When Keira missed a rotation, Maya nearly shouted from the bench but bit her tongue.

Coach glanced at her. "You see something?"

Maya hesitated. "They're leaving the weak side open."

Coach nodded. "Good eye." She turned back to the court. "Team, listen up! Watch that weak side; they're taking advantage."

The next play ran clean. Coach threw Maya a small nod.

Something flickered inside her—a reminder that leadership didn't have to stop when movement did.

After practice, Maya stayed behind again, crutches propped beside her. The ice pack was long melted, leaving her sock damp and her ankle throbbing.

Coach approached quietly, clipboard under her arm. "You did good today," she said. "Saw things most of them didn't."

Maya frowned. "Didn't feel like it. I hate sitting out."

"I know." Coach leaned against the bleachers. "But sometimes sitting out gives you perspective. You can see the whole floor from here. Use that."

Maya didn't answer right away. Her gaze drifted over the court—the scuffed paint, the faint reflection of the lights, the lines that mapped her second home. She knew every inch of it, but for the first time, it looked different.

"You think that's leadership?" Maya asked softly. "Just… watching?"

Coach smiled. "Sometimes. The best players aren't the ones who never fall. They're the ones who stay connected even when they can't move."

Maya nodded slowly, though her chest still ached with frustration.

The next few days dragged. The swelling eased, but her ankle still screamed when she turned too fast. She limped through the hallways with a brace and an ice pack tucked in her backpack.

By Wednesday, the team was prepping for the weekend tournament, and Maya was officially benched.

"You'll be back next week," Coach said. "We need you healthy, not heroic."

Maya forced a smile, but inside, she felt small. The team huddled around the clipboard, voices overlapping. Plays were drawn, roles assigned. Her name wasn't called once.

When practice ended, Janelle caught up with her. "You okay?"

Maya shrugged. "Fine."

"You sure?"

Maya hesitated. "It's weird. They're getting better, and I'm just… here."

Janelle nudged her shoulder. "You're still the voice in the room, even if you're not on the floor."

Maya wanted to believe that.

Game day arrived again, and she wore her warm-ups, ankle wrapped tight. The gym pulsed with sound—cheers, claps, sneakers squeaking in sync. She sat at the end of the bench, clipboard in hand, watching.

At first, it was agony. Every instinct screamed to run, to help, to *do*. But somewhere between the first and second quarter, something changed.

She started to see patterns others missed—the quiet gaps between defenders, the rhythm of movement, when a play was about to collapse before it did.

"Coach," she said suddenly. "We can overload left—they're biting too hard on the screens."

Coach glanced at her, then back at the court. "You sure?"

"Watch."

They did—and just like she said, the defense crumbled. The team scored.

Coach turned, eyebrows raised. "Good call, Harper."

Maya grinned. "Told you."

By the fourth quarter, Maya was calling out signals from the bench, waving hand motions to Janelle and Keira. The girls followed. Each time they scored, she clapped, loud and proud, until the whole bench caught her energy.

They won by seven.

The team rushed the court, shouting, laughing, throwing high-fives. Janelle ran straight to Maya and hugged her. "That's your win too," she said. "Coach listened to *you*."

Coach approached, smiling. "That's what I mean about perspective. You played the game without stepping on the floor."

Maya blinked back sudden tears. "Guess I can still lead from the sidelines."

"Exactly." Coach rested a hand on her shoulder. "Leadership doesn't start or stop with a whistle."

Later that night, Maya sat in her room, leg propped on a pillow, ice pressed against her ankle. Her phone buzzed nonstop—texts from teammates, photos from the game, emojis flooding in.

Janelle: u called every play right 🏀

Keira: okay okay u got skills even from the bench

Coach: proud of you today. rest that ankle.

Maya stared at the last one for a long moment before smiling. She opened her notebook, flipping past old pages of plays and quotes until she found a blank one.

At the top, she wrote:

Playing through pain isn't about ignoring it. It's about learning from it.

She tapped the pen against the page and added:

I thought swagger meant never breaking down.

But maybe swagger is how you rebuild.

The next morning, she limped into the gym with her brace still on and the same fire burning in her chest. The team was already warming up.

Coach spotted her and grinned. "Couldn't stay away?"

"Had to make sure you didn't steal my plays," Maya said.

Coach laughed. "Welcome back, Harper. You're cleared for light practice. Just no hero moves."

"Yes, ma'am."

As Maya stepped onto the court, pain still whispered through her ankle, but it didn't scare her anymore. It reminded her she was still in the game—still moving, still leading, even when it hurt.

She bounced the ball once, testing her balance. The sound echoed loud and steady.

Pain was temporary. Purpose wasn't.

CHAPTER 7

SISTERHOOD ON THE LINE

The locker room was buzzing after Friday's practice.

Music thumped from someone's speaker, laughter bounced off tile walls, and the mood was lighter than it had been in weeks. The team had started winning again—three games in a row—and the chemistry was finally clicking.

Maya could feel it in the air: the rhythm, the confidence, the quiet pride of a team beginning to believe in itself.

She sat tying her shoes when she heard the whisper.

"Did you see Bri's post last night?"

The tone was half-giggle, half-gossip.

"She really wore *that*? Girl, she needs to chill. Not everything has to be a crop top."

A chorus of low chuckles followed.

Maya looked up. Bri was sitting two benches down, her shoulders tense. She was the youngest on varsity, a sophomore with raw talent and the kind of awkward shyness that made her a target. Her hands froze mid-lace, and she tried to smile, but her eyes dropped to the floor.

Keira leaned back against her locker, smirking. "I'm just saying, we're athletes, not influencers."

A few girls laughed again, the sound echoing too loud in the small room.

Maya felt her stomach twist. She recognized that sound—it was the same one she'd heard from the boys' court months ago. The sound that made you question whether you belonged in the room at all.

She tried to stay quiet, but Bri's silence hit too close to home.

"Y'all done?" Maya said finally, her voice calm but firm.

The laughter cut short. A few heads turned.

Keira arched a brow. "Just talking."

"Yeah?" Maya stood, tightening her brace. "Because it sounds like judging."

Keira crossed her arms. "Relax. It's not that serious."

"It is when someone's sitting right there pretending not to hear it."

The room went still. Bri's eyes flicked up, wide and uncertain. Maya caught her gaze and gave the smallest nod—*you don't have to sit through this alone.*

Keira scoffed. "You always gotta play hero, huh?"

"Not hero," Maya said. "Just decent."

The words hung there for a long second, heavy but unmoving. Then Janelle spoke quietly from the other side of the room. "She's right."

One by one, a few heads nodded. Keira rolled her eyes, grabbed her bag, and muttered, "Whatever," before heading out.

The door slammed shut, leaving the air quieter than before.

After a moment, Bri mumbled, "Thanks."

Maya shook her head. "You don't have to thank me."

"I do. People talk about me all the time, and I just… let them."

"Not anymore," Maya said softly. "You don't have to."

Bri smiled weakly. "You think it ever stops? The comments, the whispers?"

Maya thought about it—the coach who told her she was too intense, the boys who laughed when she stepped on the court, the teammates who said she acted like she owned the gym.

"No," Maya said. "But you get stronger at ignoring them. Or calling them out."

The next day's game was an away match—crowded gym, loud fans, bad lighting. The kind of chaos Maya secretly loved. Her ankle was still taped, but she was back in the starting lineup.

During warmups, she noticed Bri on the edge of the court, dribbling nervously. She'd changed her pregame playlist, her focus tight and quiet.

Maya jogged over and bumped her shoulder lightly. "You ready?"

Bri smiled. "Trying to be."

"Don't try. Be."

Bri nodded, eyes steadying.

By the second quarter, the game turned rough. The other team played physical—elbows, shoves, trash talk. During a free throw, one opposing player leaned toward Bri and muttered, "You're too soft to be out here."

Maya heard it.

Bri flinched but didn't respond. She missed her next shot.

At the next timeout, Maya pulled her aside. "Don't let her in your head. You miss one shot, fine. You miss your confidence, they win."

Bri nodded, swallowing hard.

Back on the court, Maya watched her carefully. The ball swung around, hit Bri on the wing, and this time, she didn't hesitate. She drove the lane, took contact, and finished strong off the glass.

The bench erupted.

Even Coach cracked a smile. "That's the way, Bri!"

As Bri jogged back on defense, Maya caught her eye. "That's what I'm talking about," she mouthed.

After the game, they won by eight. The locker room was electric—music blasting, towels snapping, laughter bouncing off the walls.

Bri was glowing, cheeks flushed. "Did you see that drive?" she said, laughing breathlessly.

"I saw everything," Maya said. "You killed it."

Bri laughed again, but her eyes softened. "You know, before yesterday, I almost quit."

Maya blinked. "What?"

"I was tired of feeling like the extra one. Like I didn't fit."

Maya nodded slowly. "I get that."

Bri tilted her head. "You? You're like... fearless."

Maya smiled, but it was small. "Fearless doesn't mean it doesn't hurt. It just means you play through it anyway."

Bri thought for a moment, then nodded. "Then I guess I'll play through it too."

Later, as the bus rumbled back toward home, the team dozed off one by one. The hum of the highway filled the silence. Maya sat by the window, ankle propped on her backpack, watching lights blur past.

Janelle slid into the seat beside her. "You handled that like a pro."

Maya smiled faintly. "Had to. I remember what it felt like."

"Coach saw it too," Janelle said. "She told me she's proud of how you're stepping up."

Maya didn't answer right away. She just kept watching the passing lights.

Then she said quietly, "Leadership isn't just calling plays, huh?"

Janelle shook her head. "Sometimes it's calling people out."

They both laughed softly.

When the bus finally pulled up to the school parking lot, the girls gathered their bags, still sleepy but buzzing from the win.

Bri lingered near the steps, waiting for Maya. "Hey," she said. "I talked to the assistant coach. I asked if we could do something."

Maya raised an eyebrow. "What's that?"

Bri grinned. "A 'locker room code.' Like a pledge. No gossip, no body talk, no tearing each other down."

Maya blinked, surprised. "You serious?"

"Yeah. I figured if you can call it out, maybe we can stop it before it starts."

Maya grinned. "That's leadership, Bri."

Bri blushed. "Guess I learned from the best."

The next practice, Coach Ramirez called everyone in before warmups.

"Before we start," she said, "Bri's got something to share."

Bri looked nervous but held her chin high. "We talked about how we treat each other in here. This team's about respect—on the court and off. So I made something." She held up a paper with signatures across the bottom.

At the top, it read:

The Sisterhood Code: We rise together. We protect each other. We play as one.

Coach looked at Maya, then back at Bri. "I like that."

Maya stepped forward. "So do I."

One by one, every girl nodded. The team clapped, the sound echoing loud and proud.

For the first time all season, it wasn't just noise. It was unity.

That night, Maya wrote in her notebook again:

Swagger used to mean standing out.

Now it means standing up.

She smiled, closing the book.

Because for the first time, her leadership wasn't just about proving herself. It was about protecting the sisterhood that finally believed in her—and in itself.

CHAPTER 8

SWAGGER COSTS

By Monday morning, the "Sisterhood Code" hung on the locker room bulletin board in purple marker, laminated like a promise. Someone added a tiny crown above the word *protect*; someone else drew a basketball beside *play as one*. Every name was there, looping signatures layered over one another like a huddle.

Maya paused in front of it longer than she meant to. She should've felt light. Proud, even. Instead, a knot had settled under her ribs, tight as a shoelace pulled too hard.

It started as a whisper and turned into a rhythm:

Leaders don't slip. Leaders don't snap. Leaders don't get tired.

She tugged her brace tighter and pushed the feeling away.

"Captain," Janelle said, coming up behind her with a grin, "we still on for film review at lunch?"

Maya nodded. "Yeah. Corner traps and weak-side cuts."

"Look at you," Janelle teased. "All business."

Maya smirked, but it felt thin. All business meant there wasn't time for anything else.

At school, things had shifted. A group of freshmen stared as Maya passed, then burst into shy giggles. A teacher in the hallway said, "Nice win, Harper," like she'd solved a math theorem. Even the boys, the same ones who once told her the girls' court was down the hall, nodded in brief truce.

On social media, the team's account reposted game highlights with captions like **SWAGGER IN MOTION** and **HER TURN TO LEAD**. Under one clip of Maya calling rotations, the comments stacked up fast:

she's tough

future coach fr

why she yelling tho

tone it down ma'am 💀

y'all act like this is the nba

Maya scrolled, thumb hovering over the screen. She wasn't new to opinions, but visibility sharpened every edge. The praise felt slippery; the criticism stuck like burrs.

She locked her phone and slid it into her backpack as if that would quiet the noise inside her head.

Practice ran hot that afternoon. Coach Ramirez pushed their legs with full-court press drills until lungs burned. And even though the Sisterhood Code had softened the locker room edges, fatigue brought out old habits.

"Talk, talk, talk," Maya called, trying to keep everyone's feet moving and minds clear. "Heads on swivels!"

Keira glared after a missed assignment. "I *am* talking."

"Then be heard," Maya shot back.

The whistle blew. Coach clapped once, hard. "Reset. And we keep this constructive."

Keira sank into her stance, breathing sharp through her nose. Maya swallowed whatever comeback sat on her tongue. She was supposed to model the code she helped post on the wall.

After drills, as they stretched, Coach crouched beside Maya. "You're doing too much after practice?"

Maya blinked. "Like…?"

"I'm getting the sense you're carrying everything — plays, pace, people's feelings. Good leaders distribute weight."

"I'm fine."

Coach didn't smile. "Being fine and being sustainable aren't the same."

Maya nodded even as her chest tightened. She didn't know how to be less than all-in.

That night, homework stacked like bricks. A lab worksheet. Two chapters of history. An English reflection due at midnight. Her mother knocked twice and left a bowl of sliced mango on her desk.

"You look tired, baby," Mom said from the doorway.

"I'm okay."

Mom's eyes softened. "Okay isn't rest."

Maya opened her notebook anyway. The edges of the Sisterhood Code peeked out of her memory like a bookmark she couldn't ignore. She scribbled plays in the margins of her history notes. She read a paragraph and forgot it immediately. She wrote the English reflection and then deleted it, convinced it sounded like a speech. At 11:37 p.m., she finally hit submit and stared at the ceiling until sleep came in pieces.

By midweek, the cost started to show.

In the lunchroom, a younger player asked, "Can you watch my form after school?"

Another: "Can you talk to Coach about getting me more minutes?" In the hallway: "Can you repost our team flyer?" "Can you help me stretch before the game?" "Can you text the group chat?" "Can you—"

Maya said yes until her throat ran out of words.

The comments online sharpened too. A rival account clipped a moment where Maya pointed emphatically after a turnover and captioned: **Harper blames teammates for her own mistakes?** The angle made it look worse than it had been. The thread swelled:

she's a try-hard

that's not leadership

at least own ur L

Maya shut her phone, palms sweating. She set it face down, as if the glow itself accused her. Janelle slid into the seat across from her and, without a word, flipped the phone back over and put it in Maya's bag.

"Eat," she said, pushing a banana toward her. "Your hands are shaking."

"I'm fine," Maya whispered.

Janelle gave her a look. "Stop lying to the person who's with you every day."

Maya exhaled. "It's like the more I do right, the more I have to hold together."

"Then put some of it down," Janelle said. "Delegate."

"To who? Half the time I'm the only one seeing the angles."

Janelle smiled crookedly. "So teach us. That's lighter than hauling us."

The words sat with Maya for the rest of the day, turning over like a coin in her palm.

Thursday's practice was all defense. Bodies hit the floor; elbows turned rosy; the gym rang with effort. Mid-scrimmage, Bri missed a box-out and groaned.

"My bad, my bad—"

"Next play," Maya said, hand tapping Bri's shoulder. "Shoulders square; feel the hip, then release."

Bri nodded, eyes bright with attention rather than fear. Keira, watching, rolled her neck and muttered, "Teacher's pet."

Maya met her gaze. "You want this rep?"

Keira hesitated, then nodded. "Yeah."

"Take it," Maya said, stepping aside. "Teach it back."

Keira walked Bri through the footwork. It wasn't perfect, but it was honest. When the rep clicked, all three of them felt it — a small shift, like a door easing open.

Coach's whistle chirped. "There it is," she called. "That's peer leadership."

Maya let the praise pass by her and land where it belonged — with the team.

Maybe the weight wasn't meant to be carried alone. Maybe it was meant to be *shared* until everyone felt stronger holding a corner.

That evening, the cost changed shape. A DM slid into her inbox from an unknown account:

chill w ur "code." locker rooms aren't therapy. just hoop.

Maya stared at it. She typed and erased three replies. She could report it. She could ignore it. Instead, she screenshotted the message and sent it to Coach with one line:

FYI. Not engaging. Just keeping you looped.

Coach replied two minutes later:

Good choice. Your energy is precious. Guard it.

Maya put the phone down and breathed. *Guard it.* The phrase rooted itself like an anchor.

She opened her notebook and wrote:

Costs I can accept: time, sweat, sore legs, less sleep *sometimes.*

Costs I won't accept: my joy, my voice, my teammates' dignity.

She underlined the last line twice.

Friday's game was the kind that tests ceilings — packed bleachers, a drumline hammering the walls, and an opponent that loved to bait. The first quarter was a mess of whistles. By the third, the score was a snarl.

Maya felt that thin line stretch under her feet — invisible or too much — and this time she stepped onto something steadier.

"Keira, you've got next call," she said during a free throw. "See the angles. I'll echo."

Keira's eyes flicked with surprise, then squared with responsibility. She called the next defensive shift clean. Janelle mirrored. Bri picked up the backline talk. The gym noise didn't get quieter, but Maya's chest did.

With a minute left, tie game, Northside ran a high screen that Maya had seen on film. She didn't scream. She pointed once, low and quick, and Keira slid into the hedge like she'd been there for years. Turnover. Fast break. Layup. Up two.

The horn finally came like a mercy. Win by three.

They didn't dogpile. They exhaled — a long, collective breath they didn't know they'd been holding.

In the handshake line, the opposing coach nodded at Maya. "Floor general," he said simply.

Maya squeezed his hand back. "Team general," she corrected, half to him, mostly to herself.

Back in the locker room, sweat still cooling on their skin, Coach pointed at the laminated Code.

"You wrote it on the wall," she said. "You wrote it louder on the floor."

She looked at Maya. "Leadership will always cost you something. Be wise about what you spend."

Maya nodded. The knot under her ribs loosened at last.

When the others filtered out — singing, joking, tossing tape balls at a trash can that missed every time — Maya lingered. The overhead light caught the laminate and made the purple ink glow.

She pulled a Sharpie from her bag and added a small line at the bottom, tiny but bold:

We carry this together.

She capped the marker and stepped back. The sentence looked right — like the missing piece of a play finally drawn in.

As she slung her bag over her shoulder, she heard the thud of a ball in the empty gym. The sound traveled through the wall and into her bones, steady as a heartbeat.

Swagger did cost. It always would.

But if the price was distributed — if the team held corners, if the joy stayed intact — then she could afford it.

She opened the door and let the echo follow her out into the hall, the night air cool against her face, the weight on her shoulders lighter than it had been all week.

Not because she was carrying less.

Because she wasn't carrying it alone.

CHAPTER 9

THE UNDERDOG GAME

Tournament day began with thunder in the distance and nerves that hummed like static. The team bus rattled down the freeway, wipers slicing drizzle from the windshield. Inside, music blasted low through shared earbuds, candy wrappers crinkled, and every conversation hovered between focus and fear.

Maya sat near the back, notebook open on her knees, sketching the opponent's tendencies from film: strong corners, sloppy baseline defense, guards who over-commit on hedges. Across the aisle, Janelle leaned over.

"You always study like it's finals week," she teased.

"It *is* finals week," Maya said without looking up, "and this game's worth more credit."

Janelle laughed. "Just don't burn out before tip-off, professor."

Coach Ramirez rose from her seat at the front, steady even as the bus bounced. "Ladies," she called, "remember—no one expects us to win this one. Good. That means we play loose, play smart, and make them remember our names. Harper, you've got floor reads. Keep us steady."

Maya nodded, pulse quickening. The words *no one expects us to win* didn't scare her. They fueled her.

The gym in Clearview smelled of popcorn and tension. The home crowd packed both sides of the bleachers, blue shirts blending into a single wall of noise. The scoreboard glowed 0–0, a blank stage.

Warm-ups went crisp—passes snapping, sneakers squealing. Bri nailed three jumpers in a row; Keira grinned for the first time all week. But when the buzzer sounded and the announcer's voice boomed their names, the crowd drowned them out with chants: *Underdogs. Underdogs.*

Maya exhaled through her nose. *Let them bark. We bite.*

The tip went up; the ball came down in her hands.

She pushed tempo, calling "Motion two!" before the defense settled. The first possession ended with Janelle's floater kissing glass. Two points. The bench jumped.

But Clearview answered fast—three-pointer, steal, transition layup. The scoreboard blinked 5–2 before a minute passed.

Coach signaled timeout. The huddle tightened. Sweat already beaded on foreheads.

"They're baiting us," Coach said. "Harper, slow it down. Make them defend longer than they want to."

"Yes, Coach."

When play resumed, Maya controlled the rhythm—twenty seconds of ball movement, patience that annoyed the home crowd. On cue, she slipped a pass to Bri on the back cut. Layup. Tie game.

The first quarter ended 14–14. No one had expected parity. The whispers in the stands quieted.

By halftime, Clearview led by five, but their faces showed frustration. Every possession was a war of will. In the locker room, Coach handed Maya the dry-erase marker.

"Your read."

Maya stepped to the board, adrenaline humming behind her ribs. "They collapse hard on our drives. We bait it, then kick to Bri or Janelle for corner threes. Keira—seal early; they're slow rotating back."

Heads nodded. For once, no one doubted her. Not Coach. Not teammates.

When the buzzer called them back, the hallway smelled of popcorn and possibility.

The third quarter was a blur of bodies and breath. Clearview's pressure increased; whistles multiplied. Maya took a charge that rattled her teeth. She hit the floor, pain flashing up her spine, but stayed down only a second before Coach's voice cut through: "You good?"

"Always," she grunted, standing. The ref gave her the ball.

Next play, she drained a mid-range jumper that silenced half the gym.

Then came the run.

Janelle hit back-to-back threes. Keira blocked a shot so clean it echoed. Bri dove for a loose ball, slid across the floor, and kicked it to Maya, who finished through contact. The whistle shrieked—*and one.*

Maya hit the free throw. Score: 43–41, Spirit High up by two.

The bench roared. Coach clenched her fist instead of shouting; she didn't have to.

In the fourth, fatigue hit like a wave. Maya's ankle barked with every cut. The home crowd grew desperate, chanting louder, stomping bleachers until the floor vibrated.

Clearview tied it with a minute left. 56–56.

Timeout.

The team circled Coach, lungs heaving.

"They'll expect isolation," Coach said. "So we give them misdirection. Maya—set the screen instead of taking it. Let Bri drive. Trust the shift."

Maya blinked. "You sure?"

Coach smiled. "Sometimes leadership means giving the spotlight away."

Maya nodded. "Got it."

They broke the huddle with hands stacked. "One stop, one score, one voice," Maya said.

The girls echoed it softly—"One voice"—and took the court.

The play unfolded in slow motion. Maya dribbled at the top, eyes scanning. She passed right, then cut across the key and planted for the screen. The defender chased her, leaving Bri a lane.

Bri drove hard, bounced off contact, and flipped the layup high off glass. *Swish.*

The clock: 6.8 seconds.

Clearview inbounded, sprinting the length of the court. A shot went up at the buzzer—long, arcing, heart-stopping.

It rimmed out.

The horn blared.

For a heartbeat, the gym went still. Then chaos.

The bench erupted, bodies colliding in laughter and disbelief. Maya fell backward into Janelle's arms, both screaming over the noise.

They had done it. The underdogs had just taken down the number-one seed.

Later, when the bleachers emptied and the noise faded, Maya sat on the floor near center court, legs outstretched, staring at the scoreboard still frozen at 58–56.

Coach walked over, folding her arms. "How's the ankle?"

"Alive," Maya said. "Barely."

Coach chuckled. "You screened the winning play on that thing."

Maya grinned. "Guess it's tougher than it looks."

Coach crouched beside her. "You led exactly how I hoped you would—strategic, composed, generous. That's the kind of captain colleges remember."

Maya blinked. "You think so?"

"I know so. But more important—you made them believe in themselves."

Maya looked toward her teammates dancing in the corner for a team selfie, arms tangled, laughter spilling everywhere. "They made it easy to believe back," she said.

Coach nodded, eyes shining with something close to pride. "Get some ice. Tomorrow, we prep for the final."

On the bus ride home, the air buzzed with victory songs. The team chanted *Her turn! Her turn!* until Maya's cheeks hurt from smiling. But beneath the joy, she felt something deeper settle inside her—calm, certain, earned.

She leaned her forehead against the window, watching raindrops streak past the reflection of her face.

Months ago, she'd fought to prove she belonged.

Weeks ago, she'd learned to share the floor.

Tonight, she'd discovered another truth: swagger wasn't about standing at the front.

It was about stepping aside when the team needed space to rise.

She pulled out her notebook and, under her last entry, wrote:

Swagger isn't always visible. Sometimes it's the quiet move that changes every-thing.

Janelle leaned over the seat. "Coach says interviews at school tomorrow. You ready, star?"

Maya smiled. "Tell them it wasn't me. It was us."

"Sure," Janelle said, grinning. "But they're still gonna ask how it feels to win the underdog game."

Maya looked out the window again, raindrops glimmering like confetti.

"It feels," she said softly, "like the start of something bigger."

CHAPTER 10

HER TURN TO LEAD

Saturday morning dawned gray and breathless, the kind of sky that looked like it was holding its breath. The championship banner already hung across the gym's rafters, waiting for new names. The stands filled with faces — parents, classmates, local reporters — the hum of anticipation thick enough to taste.

Maya sat at her locker, lacing her shoes slow and deliberate. The chatter around her blurred. She could hear only the steady rhythm of her breath and the echo of the last words Coach had said before they left the bus:

"We've come too far to play small now. But remember — leading doesn't mean carrying everything. It means trusting what you've built."

She looked at the laminated Sisterhood Code on the wall:

We rise together. We protect each other. We play as one.

The purple ink shimmered faintly in the fluorescent light.

She touched the edge of the poster with her fingertips. *We play as one.*

That's what today would mean.

The gym roared when they ran out. The other team, Eastfield High, was everything they'd heard — fast, tall, confident, undefeated. They didn't bother hiding their smirks during warmups.

"Let them underestimate us," Janelle whispered. "That's when we hit hardest."

Maya smiled. "That's the plan."

When the whistle blew for tip-off, everything inside her sharpened. The ball arced high, caught sunlight through the skylight, and came down into chaos.

From the first possession, the pace was brutal. Bodies collided, sneakers screamed against the court. Maya could feel the old burn in her ankle, but she stayed steady — voice calm, eyes scanning, mind moving faster than fear.

"2-3 zone! Push baseline!" she shouted, and the team responded like choreography. Pass, pivot, swing.

Janelle in the corner — three-pointer.

Swish.

The crowd roared.

By halftime, the score was tied 31–31. In the locker room, the air was thick with heat and breath. Coach Ramirez stood near the whiteboard, arms crossed, sweat glinting on her brow.

"You're matching them shot for shot," she said. "But the next sixteen minutes are mental. They're waiting for you to break focus."

Her eyes met Maya's. "Keep the pace. Keep the trust."

Maya nodded, wiping her face with her towel. The team leaned in close, heads touching, the smell of sweat and adrenaline binding them together.

"Let's write the ending ourselves," Maya said quietly.

The third quarter tested everything.

Eastfield's star guard turned ruthless, cutting through defenders like a blade. Bri got hit with a hard screen and fell, wincing. Keira missed two rebounds in a row. The scoreboard tilted 44–38, Eastfield's lead growing.

Maya's chest ached. The noise from the stands turned sharp — whistles, chants, taunts. She could feel panic rising like static.

Timeout.

Coach motioned them in.

"Breathe," she said first. "Don't chase the game. Make it come to you."

Maya's eyes darted to Bri, clutching her knee. "You good?"

Bri grimaced. "Hurts, but I can go."

Maya hesitated, then shook her head. "No. Sit. You earned your rest. We'll finish what you started."

Coach studied her, then nodded. "That's leadership."

When play resumed, something shifted. Maya slowed everything down. Instead of forcing plays, she let the rhythm unfold — like she was conducting more than competing.

She called for Keira to post inside. Fake right, pivot left, bank off glass. Bucket. Next possession — Janelle cut baseline, Maya fed her clean through the gap.

Layup.

The scoreboard closed: 46–45.

And then came the silence before the storm.

Fourth quarter. Two minutes left. Tie game again.

Coach didn't need to call a play this time. Maya already had one ready — drawn weeks ago in her notebook, scribbled in pen beside a quote she'd written to herself: *Play like you already belong.*

She dribbled up the court, heart pounding steady with the bounce. The defense shadowed tight. She motioned to Janelle — flare screen, left wing. Then she faked the pass, spun through a trap, and pulled up midrange.

The ball left her hands in perfect rotation—the kind of shot that felt right before it landed. *Swish.*

The crowd exploded.

Coach yelled, "Back! Back!" but Maya was already sprinting, eyes locked on the ball. The opponent's guard drove, panicked, and forced a pass that Keira intercepted clean.

Clock: 7 seconds.

Maya caught the outlet and dribbled, not to score, but to *wait.* She'd learned the difference. Four… three… two…

The buzzer blared.

58–56.

They'd done it again.

The gym erupted. The bench emptied. The noise was too big to hold in one heart. Janelle tackled her in a hug; Bri limped over, laughing through tears. The crowd chanted *Spirit! Spirit!* until it became thunder.

When the trophy was handed to Coach Ramirez, she didn't lift it first. She turned to Maya. "This one's yours," she said, voice soft but certain. "You earned it."

Maya shook her head. "*We* did."

Coach smiled. "Exactly."

The flashbulbs caught the moment — Maya holding the trophy high, teammates swarming around her, a storm of joy and sweat and disbelief. The noise faded into something deeper: belonging.

Later, after the crowd had spilled out and the gym went quiet again, Maya wandered back onto the court alone. The floor was sticky with victory confetti.

She stood at center court, the same spot where she'd once whispered, *If they won't listen, I'll show them.*

She smiled. *I did.*

Her notebook was still in her bag, pages filled with plays, quotes, and fragments of thought. She flipped to a blank page, sat cross-legged, and began to write.

Leadership isn't a title. It's a trust.

It's knowing when to speak, when to listen, and when to hand the ball to someone else.

Swagger used to be about proving them wrong. Now it's about proving us right.

She stared at the last line, then added one more:

Today wasn't just my turn to lead. It was our turn to rise.

As she left, the lights dimmed automatically, leaving only the faint glow from the scoreboard, still frozen on their final numbers. She paused at the door and looked back one last time.

Tomorrow, the headlines would have her name in them.

But in her heart, she knew the real story belonged to all of them — the girls who were told to quiet down, to stay small, to let someone else run the court.

They hadn't just played a championship game. They'd rewritten the playbook.

Maya reached for the switch, then stopped. She let the lights stay on, spilling across the polished wood, the nets still swaying from the last shot.

"Leave them shining," she murmured. "Let the next girl see what's possible."

And as the door closed behind her, the words of the Sisterhood Code seemed to hum in the still air:

We rise together. We protect each other. We play as one

CHAPTER 11

RESPECT, NOT PERMISSION

The school's trophy case gleamed brighter that Monday morning. The gold plate under the newest prize still read **PENDING ENGRAVING**, but the reflection of victory shone clear enough.

Students stopped Maya in the hallway—high-fives, selfies, a few autograph jokes—but she felt oddly weightless, like she'd left part of herself back on that court.

"Captain Harper!" one senior boy called. "Future WNBA, right?"

She laughed, shaking her head. "Let's pass biology first."

Everyone wanted a piece of her confidence now. It was strange—how the same energy once called *too much* had turned into something people wanted to borrow.

That afternoon, Coach Ramirez called a brief meeting in the gym. Reporters from the *Houston Chronicle* were setting up near the bleachers; flashes popped against the polished floor.

"Interviews," Coach said, handing Maya a water bottle. "They asked for you."

Maya wiped her palms on her warm-ups. "Me? Not the whole team?"

"They'll get the team later," Coach said. "But you—you're the story. Just remember who you represent."

Maya nodded. The reminder didn't scare her; it steadied her.

The reporter—a woman with a notepad and calm, curious eyes—smiled as Maya sat down across from her.

"Congratulations," she said. "Underdog champions. How's it feel?"

Maya hesitated. "Loud," she said finally. "But the kind of loud that feels earned."

The reporter chuckled. "I like that. Tell me, what changed for this team?"

Maya glanced toward her teammates joking by the water fountain. "We stopped asking for permission. To play our way. To lead our way. Once we did that, everything opened up."

The reporter's pen scratched quickly. "Sounds like swagger."

Maya grinned. "The quiet kind."

When the article came out two days later, the headline read:

"Maya Harper and the Spirit of Swagger: Respect Rewritten."

The piece went viral locally. Teachers printed copies; girls from the junior-high team asked for selfies at lunch. Even Coach's stoic expression cracked into a proud half-smile.

But not every comment was praise.

Online threads buzzed again.

She's good but cocky.

Let's see if she keeps it up next season.

All this for high-school ball?

Maya scrolled, her chest tightening the way it used to before games. She shut the screen and reminded herself: *Respect doesn't come from clicks. It comes from consistency.*

She set her phone face-down and went outside to shoot alone.

The court behind the school was nearly empty at sunset. The air smelled of cut grass and distant barbecue smoke. She bounced the ball once, twice, listening to the echo fade into evening.

Janelle showed up ten minutes later, hoodie zipped to her chin.

"Knew I'd find you here."

Maya smiled faintly. "Old habits."

Janelle leaned against the fence. "Everyone's talking about you. Even the principal called you 'our hometown hero.'"

Maya rolled her eyes. "Yeah, and half of social media called me overrated."

"You really still read that stuff?"

"Trying not to." She took a shot—rimmed out. "I thought winning would fix it, you know? The doubt."

Janelle caught the rebound, passed it back. "It doesn't fix it. It just changes who doubts you. Before it was others. Now it's you."

Maya stopped dribbling, letting the truth sink in. "So what fixes it?"

Janelle grinned. "Playing again. Always does."

They stayed until the streetlights flickered on, trading shots and stories, laughter cutting through the hum of the night.

By Friday, normalcy tried to return. Quizzes, group projects, morning announcements. But the world outside basketball still looked at Maya differently—like everything she did now had weight.

In English class, the teacher read a quote aloud:

"Leadership is not about being in charge. It's about caring for those in your charge."

Without meaning to, Maya smiled. She scribbled it into her notebook beside her old plays.

After class, Bri caught up to her. "Hey, you free after school? I'm helping the JV girls run drills. Coach said you could stop by if you want."

Maya hesitated. "JV?"

"Yeah. They're nervous. First tournament this weekend."

She remembered her own first year—too small jersey, too big dreams, the sting of laughter when she missed easy shots.

"Yeah," she said. "I'll come."

The JV gym was smaller, dimmer, but full of energy. Ten girls lined up along the baseline, eyes wide when Maya walked in.

"She's here!" one whispered.

Coach Wilson, their assistant, grinned. "Girls, this is Maya Harper—"

"—We know," they said in unison, making her laugh.

She clapped her hands. "Alright then. Let's hoop."

They ran passing drills first, then defensive slides. Every few minutes, she stopped to correct a stance or offer a high-five. The girls hung on every word.

Halfway through, one of them—a thin-shouldered freshman—tripped on a shuffle and fell. Her cheeks flushed bright red.

"Sorry," the girl muttered. "I'm just clumsy."

Maya crouched beside her. "You're not clumsy. You're learning."

The girl nodded, eyes wet. "Everyone laughs when I mess up."

Maya smiled gently. "Then they forgot what it feels like to start."

The girl wiped her face, stood, and got back in line. By the next round, her movements were sharper.

Watching her, Maya felt something shift again—something deeper than victory. Respect wasn't about headlines. It was about moments like this: helping someone else believe they belonged.

When practice ended, Coach Wilson pulled Maya aside.

"You've got a gift," she said. "Not just playing—teaching."

Maya laughed softly. "Guess it's contagious."

Wilson smiled. "So what's next for you, Captain Harper?"

Maya looked at the polished court, the dust rising from sneakers, the energy pulsing through every echo.

"Maybe more of this," she said. "Lifting others up. Building something bigger than just a game."

That weekend, she found herself back at the big-team gym for open practice. No crowd, no reporters, just squeaks, breath, and rhythm.

Coach Ramirez walked in mid-drill, clipboard in hand.

"You never rest, do you?"

Maya smiled. "Resting's overrated."

Coach shook her head, amused. "College scouts called. They'll want film. But whatever happens next, remember—your value isn't measured by offers."

"I know," Maya said. "Respect, not permission."

Coach blinked, then smiled. "Exactly."

Later, after the lights dimmed and the team filed out, Maya stayed behind again—alone, ball balanced on her fingertips.

She thought about every label she'd worn: *too much, too loud, too bossy.*

And every one she'd earned: *leader, mentor, champion.*

She realized both were fuel. Without the first, she might never have chased the second.

The doors creaked, and Bri peeked in. "You coming?"

"In a sec."

Bri grinned. "Don't stay all night, legend."

Maya chuckled, shooting one last jumper. The ball swished clean.

As it rolled back to her feet, she whispered, "Respect earned."

She looked around the empty gym—the same space that had once made her feel small—and felt something new: stillness, yes, but also freedom.

She no longer needed to prove she belonged here. She *was* here.

She didn't need anyone's permission.

Just purpose.

That night, back home, she flipped open her notebook again. The margins were crowded with phrases now, each one a marker of how far she'd come. At the bottom of the page, she wrote:

Respect isn't given. It's grown—play by play, choice by choice.

And the strongest leaders don't demand it. They inspire it.

She put the pen down and smiled.

Tomorrow, there would be more work—new drills, new players to lift, new voices to amplify.

But tonight, for the first time, she let herself rest.

The court could wait until morning.

It knew her name now.

CHAPTER 12

SWAGGER REDEFINED

The first day of spring tryouts smelled like new sneakers, floor polish, and nervous energy. The banners from last season still hung high above the gym — *DISTRICT CHAMPIONS, REGIONAL FINALISTS, SPIRIT HIGH SCHOOL LADY HAWKS* — reminders of what had been earned and what still waited.

Maya stood by the scorer's table, clipboard in hand. Her ankle brace was gone now, replaced by the faintest scar and a stronger stride. Coach Ramirez had invited her to help with drills — "assistant leadership," she'd called it.

Maya didn't have a title, but she didn't need one anymore.

Across the court, a group of wide-eyed freshmen stretched, sneakers squeaking as they fumbled with layups. One of them — a tiny girl with bright pink laces and too-big shorts — missed three shots in a row and hung her head.

Maya walked over, bouncing a spare ball.

"Hey," she said gently. "You always this hard on yourself, or is today special?"

The girl looked up, startled, then laughed shyly. "I'm just bad."

Maya grinned. "Nah. You're just early."

She handed her the ball. "Try again. Breathe. Bend your knees like you mean it."

The girl did — swish.

Her face lit up. "I made it!"

Maya nodded. "You did the work. Keep it."

Coach blew the whistle. "Baseline! Let's move!"

As the new players jogged to the line, Maya caught sight of Janelle, now the returning senior captain, leading warmups with her usual grin. Bri stood near the back, still wrapping her knee, cracking jokes to calm the rookies.

Watching them felt like watching her own reflection grow wider — leadership replicated, multiplied.

Coach called her over. "You still thinking about that sports management major?"

Maya smiled. "Yeah. Thinking about coaching someday, too."

Coach raised an eyebrow. "Someday? You're already doing it."

Maya laughed. "Just trying to follow good examples."

Coach chuckled, shaking her head. "You know, when I first met you, I thought you were going to break every rule I set."

"I did," Maya said, smiling. "But I rebuilt a few, too."

Coach's laughter echoed through the gym. "You sure did."

Tryouts rolled on. The gym buzzed with sneakers, whistles, and dreams in motion. The young players glanced at Maya often, mimicking her stance, her focus, her calm.

It hit her then — the full circle of it all.

Last year, she'd been the outsider trying to prove she belonged. Now she was the example others were studying. Her voice wasn't the loudest in the gym anymore, but when she spoke, people listened.

Not because she demanded it.

Because she'd earned it.

After practice, the air outside was heavy with Houston humidity, sunlight catching the rim of the bleachers like fire. The team lingered, laughing and trading stories about missed shots and inside jokes.

Bri called out, "Yo, Harper! You gonna give the newbies a speech or what?"

The freshmen perked up, eyes wide. Maya froze mid-step, laughing nervously. "A speech? Nah."

"C'mon!" Janelle said. "You're the reason half of them even tried out."

Maya looked at their expectant faces — curious, hopeful, hungry for something real. She took a breath, then climbed the first bleacher step and turned toward them.

"Alright," she said, voice steady. "Here's what I wish someone told me my first day."

The chatter faded.

"Swagger isn't noise," she began. "It's not about who shouts the loudest or who gets the most likes. It's not about perfect hair, perfect shoes, or a perfect game. It's what's left when all that fades."

She glanced toward the banners overhead.

"It's the work you do when nobody's watching. The respect you give when no one demands it. It's getting up after you fall — and helping the next person up with you."

The gym was quiet except for the sound of the ceiling fans whirring.

Maya smiled. "So when people say you've got swagger, don't let them shrink what that means. Swagger's not a show. It's your belief in yourself — the kind that doesn't need permission."

She stepped down from the bleacher. "Now get water before Coach starts suicides."

Laughter broke the silence. The girls scattered toward the fountain, shoulders lighter, smiles wider.

Coach Ramirez walked by, arms folded but eyes shining. "You know," she said quietly, "that might've been the best speech I never asked for."

Maya grinned. "Guess it's my turn to lead."

That evening, the gym emptied except for her. The golden light slanted across the floor, catching every scuff and reflection like memories. She sat on the center circle again — same spot, new story.

Her notebook was nearly full now, its pages dog-eared and smudged with pencil marks and sweat. She flipped to the back cover, running her thumb over the creases.

Every chapter of her journey lived here — pain, pressure, pride, purpose.

She wrote slowly, the final entry:

Swagger isn't defiance. It's presence.

It's walking into any space and knowing you belong — even if nobody else has ever stood there before.

It's standing up for others, standing firm for yourself, and standing tall no matter how many times they tell you to sit down.

It's resilience in motion.

She paused, listening to the hum of the air vents — the only applause she needed.

It's not about me anymore. It's about the next girl who looks at the court and thinks, maybe there's room for me too.

Maya signed her initials at the bottom — *M.H.* — then closed the notebook for the last time.

Outside, the evening smelled like rain. She stepped onto the blacktop, dribbling absently, the ball echoing off the quiet school walls. In the distance, thunder rolled — the same sound that had started the season months ago.

Back then, it had sounded like challenge.

Now, it sounded like applause.

She smiled, spinning the ball on her finger before tucking it under her arm. Her reflection shimmered faintly in a puddle nearby — taller, calmer, sure.

She whispered, "Her turn," and felt the words settle deep, not just in her, but in everything around her — the air, the echoes, the game itself.

The next morning, Maya woke early and found a message from Coach Ramirez waiting in her inbox.

Subject: Next Step

Maya,

I sent your highlights and leadership reel to a few college programs. They're interested — not just in your stats, but in your story. You've turned swagger into something teachable.

Proud doesn't even cover it.

—Coach R.

Maya smiled. Her story wasn't finished — it was just expanding.

She texted Janelle:

6AM practice tomorrow? One more for the road.

Janelle replied instantly:

you never rest 😄

nah, Maya wrote back. **just lead.**

When she reached the gym again that morning, the sun hadn't even risen. But she didn't need light to find her way anymore.

She bounced the ball once — crisp, confident, the sound of everything she'd learned: discipline, courage, grace.

And as that echo filled the quiet, she whispered her own closing line, meant not for the world but for herself:

"Swagger isn't about being seen. It's about being certain."

Then she smiled, squared her shoulders, and began to play.

AFTERWARDS

AUTHOR'S NOTE

By Joyce Lee

When I began writing *Swagger Wars II: Her Turn*, I wasn't just telling another basketball story. I was telling the story of every girl who's ever been told she's *too much* — too loud, too confident, too opinionated, too ambitious — when all she was doing was showing up as herself.

Maya Harper's journey began on a court, but her real opponent was never the scoreboard. It was the doubt that surrounds girls who lead differently. It was the whisper that says, "Know your place." Through her, I wanted to show that swagger isn't arrogance; it's *assurance.* It's believing in your value even when the world hasn't caught up yet.

Like the other titles in *The Spirit Collection: Resilience in Print*, this story connects back to real classrooms and real challenges. For me, *Her Turn* isn't just fiction — it's a reflection of what I see in schools every day. The same resilience that helps a student sink a free throw is the resilience it takes to walk into class without shame, without judgment, and without fear of being seen for what you lack instead of who you are.

Every book in this collection supports **Spirit, Inc.,** our Houston-based nonprofit working to end hygiene poverty among students. Through our **Pads & Power Initiative**, we're making sure that no girl ever has to sit out of school — or out of life — because she lacks access to something as basic as soap, deodorant, or menstrual care.

The goal has always been bigger than distribution. It's dignity. It's the quiet power that comes from being able to stand tall, clean, and confident — ready to learn, to play, to lead.

In *Her Turn*, Maya learns that leadership isn't about who shouts loudest; it's about who lifts others when the noise fades. That same truth drives the mission behind every Spirit hygiene kit and every literacy event we organize: when one of us rises, we make room for others to rise too.

If this story made you think, made you remember a time you doubted yourself, or made you want to cheer for someone finding her voice — then it did its job. And if it inspired you to act — to donate, to volunteer, or to see students in your community with new compassion — then together, we've already won something far greater than a game.

Thank you for reading, for believing, and for helping us prove that confidence — real confidence — begins with dignity.

With love and purpose,

Joyce Lee

Founder & President, *Spirit, Inc.*

Creator of *The Spirit Collection: Resilience in Print*

Houston, Texas

ABOUT THE AUTHOR

Joyce Lee is the Founder and President of **Spirit, Inc.**, a Houston-based 501(c)(3) non-profit dedicated to ending hygiene poverty and restoring dignity for *all* students—girls and boys alike—across the Greater Houston region. Through programs like **Pads & Power**, which equips girls with menstrual and hygiene essentials, and **SWAG Packs (Strength With Access & Growth)**, which supports boys with confidence and self-care resources, Spirit helps students show up ready to learn, lead, and thrive.

Joyce is also the creator of **The Spirit Collection: Resilience in Print**, a youth-literacy series that funds hygiene dignity initiatives through storytelling. Her work unites advocacy, education, and empowerment—proving that confidence begins with access, and resilience begins with voice.

🌐 **www.spirit-np.info**

spiritempowerment21@gmail.com

#PadsAndPower

#SWAGPacks

#ResilienceInPrint